Nightmares

Adventures of The Three Wings, Volume 1

Janblu Iden Ayre

Published by Janblu Iden Ayre, 2024.

This is a work of fiction. Similarities to real people, places, or events are entirely coincidental.

NIGHTMARES

First edition. October 5, 2024.

Written by Janblu Iden Ayre.

Table of Contents

Scholar's Note

A series of accounts of The Three Wings adventures has been found in Aiva's collection, recovered memories from databanks, as well as restored memories. These are separate to the accounts found within "The Creation, Rise, and Fall of The Three Wings", and do not play as important of a role in the story of The Three Wings. That being said, many scholars have found these interesting as further studies into The Three Wings, and especially as these take place in the time period that the 13 anthologies do not cover.

"Adventures of The Three Wings" is what these are being called. They are very disjointed, as we are not able to recover them in any sort of chronological order, and it would be impossible to completely organise them that way. While we can deduce roughly when they happened in relation to the formation of The Three Wings, there is still a lot missing in terms of specific dates and times. A rough marking of time will be made at the start of each 'adventure' for guidance.

Fortunately for us, the adventures have had more freedom with who is narrating. This has allowed us more insight into The Three Wings, and has given us more flexibility when preparing each text for publication.

As this is the first of the "Adventures of The Three Wings", the Scholars have prepared a longer introduction than usual. We apologise for that.

Time after the formation of The Three Wings: 3 years.

Jacob

It was the weekend and nothing of interest had happened for a few days in a row, which made me feel very nervous. I had gotten used to a constant rhythm of villainy plaguing the city over and over, so now it felt weird to just be at home doing nothing. What's more, my girlfriend was doing her final exams at school, which meant I had no-one to really hang out with. Man I missed her.

I'd thought about doing some training, but the idea was not very appealing, at least at the start. But now, feeling a little antsy, I needed to do something. I considered my options. There was always training alone, using the new automated training systems. But, if I was being honest, they made me nervous. The next options was training with Janar, but he outright scared me during training, and I wasn't looking to get my ass beat. Besides, I didn't know where he was. So that left one final option.

The prospect of convincing my other friend into doing some training was not very tempting, but the other options were worse, so I reluctantly went in search for him. Most likely, he'd be at his workship, which was located several floors in the Tower X below my floor, or my apartment as I thought of it. We used to be much closer, just a flight of stairs away, but with the new training area that had been added to the Tower X, I was suddenly tempted to take the elevator.

"Well, if I'm going to train, I might as well take the stairs," I thought as I reached out to call the elevator. Sighing, I pulled away, walking instead to the stairway to my right. There, I began to descend the stairs. I always enjoyed going down a flight of

stairs, since I normally moved so quick that it felt as though I was on the verge of falling the rest of the way. This time was no exception.

"Except this isn't quick. Come on Jacob, you can do better!" A mental trap had been laid, and I was annoyed by the fact that I'd set it off. Now, feeling guilty, I called upon my speed. My power. Without a frame of reference, I couldn't be sure if I was moving any faster or not, since my reaction time also sped up alongside my body. Normally it made everything look as though it was moving very slightly slowly, but when all you could see were boring tea green walls, everything looked normal.

That did not mean I wasn't using my power. I could feel it, a sort of tugging from within me as my energy was used to make myself go fast. Like how you know you're using your muscles when exercising, except this was a secret muscle that was attached to your soul or something. That on top of the regular strain on my leg muscles. It was a feeling that I could barely comprehend, though I knew both my friends had a better understanding of it.

It didn't take me long to reach the floor. There was a very, very small room that allowed enough space for access to the elevator and stairs, as well as one beautiful mahogany door. Making sure that I'd returned to normal speed, I approached the door and knocked.

No response. I knocked again, announcing my arrival, "Cain? Are you there?"

"I'm kinda busy here!" Cain called from the other side.

"Dude, I haven't seen you in 2 days!" I responded, twisting the door handle and letting myself into the workshop.

"Please," Cain scoffed, "You and I both know that's not a long period of time for me."

The workshop was fairly new, and so it was pretty empty. It was a large room, like a sort of living room really, with a few tables and some office chairs. There were some cabinets along the walls, and two doors, one on the left and one on the right. In the left corner furthest away from me was a massive worktable that bent in an L shape. Cain's pride and joy. He was at it, hunched over some project, completely ignoring the office chair next to him.

"Look, I was thinking-"

"Congratulations!"

"-that we could do some training!"

Cain stopped what he was doing and turned around to look at me. He did not look impressed.

"Really? That's what you interrupt me for. Training?"

"It will be good for us!" I argued.

"No, see, this will be good for us. See, it's a little machine, hard to hit but can pack quite a punch. I hope," Cain gestured at the mess on the workbench beside him. On it was what I could only describe as a mess of wires, vines, wood, metal, and circuits.

I raised my eyebrow, "Where are we going to use it?"

"In the training rooms, see!" Cain cheerfully responded. I grinned at the irony of that statement, which Cain hadn't yet grasped.

"The training rooms we don't ever use?" I asked. Cain's eyes suddenly dropped to the ground.

"Hmpf. Fine, I guess some combat training is in order," Cain admitted. He gave one solemn glance at his project, before making his way over to me. I retreated from the door to allow

Cain through, making sure to keep my eye on him lest he decide to retreat back to his project. Fortunately for us, he decided to keep following me.

Cain headed straight for the elevator, but I tugged at his arm and pulled him away. He gave me a strange look, before realisation dawned in his eyes.

"No, you're not doing this," Cain protested.

"If we're training, we're training all the way!" I confirmed, "Come on, we're taking the stairs."

I dragged Cain along with me towards the staircase to the left, the one from which I'd come from. He reluctantly let me pull him along, but made sure to make every sound of complaint he knew as we ascended the stairs. It was like every single step had personally offended him, and he was doing his best to ensure that I knew that fact.

Eventually, after much complaining, we made it to the top. Cain let out a sigh of relief as, instead of turning to continue ascending the stairs, we instead walked forward towards the big, empty room that made up the training floor. I imagined that that relief would be short-lived.

The training room was surprisingly big, feeling like an empty warehouse. In any normal skyscraper, they would have had dozens of offices in this space, or a fully featured gym. Perhaps even a well-stocked department store. It almost made me forget where I was, but it also allowed me to appreciate the Tower X for how many things one could fit inside of it without feat of the structure falling. There were benefits of living in what was essentially a giant tree crammed with tech.

"Alright then, what would you like to do?" Cain asked as he approached a hole in the floor, from which a cylindrical panel was emerging. There was a console of sorts on top of the panel, sleek and modern with touch input, though there was also a physical keyboard attached.

"I was thinking a dual would do nicely," I suggested.

Cain grimaced, "How lovely. I assume you'd like a terrain that plays to both our strengths?"

"Do a city street, a nice one."

Cain started typing furiously into the console, and the entire room around me rumbled. Concrete structures began to grow out of the ground. To the untrained eye, the growth could have been mistaken for nanomachines, but having seen Cain's powers, I knew otherwise. To me, it seemed more like a timelapse of some highly complex plant growing, which in essence was the truth of the matter. But still, the results were a convincing imitation of regular building materials.

Within a few minutes, the room had gone from being an empty space, to becoming an accurate portrayal of a nice street you could potentially find in the city. Two car lanes, with bike lanes on each side. A raised pedestrian path with plenty of space and lined with a mix of Acacia and Fig trees. Empty buildings on all sides. A fire hydrant, in classic red. Streetlights. The road even had well-thought-out drainage.

"Actually, this might be nicer than any street in the city," I thought.

Cain stepped away from the control panel, which dropped back into the ground. We were both surrounded by the street, and facing each other from either side.

"Well, ready?" Cain called.

"As always. First to give up loses?"

"Sure, works for me."

"Ready then?"

Cain nodded.

"Okay, on three then. One, two... three!"

Immediately, I jumped backwards as the trees on either side of me swung down at me. I narrowly managed to avoid the branches and leaves, and found myself backed up against a building, out of the trees reach. But if I knew anything about Cain's trees, I wouldn't be out of reach for long.

Cain simply stood on his side of the street, watching me carefully. He appeared to be doing nothing, but I could see the little seeds and circuits flowing out of the multitudes of pockets in his clothes, already assembling some kind of nature-tech abomination behind his back. All the trees on my side of the street were leaning in my direction, waiting for something to happen.

I decided to stop delaying and launch my counter-attack. There was water in those trees, and I needed it. Like an extension of myself, I reached out to that water and commanded it. Droplets of water began to form along the leaves of the trees, dripping out slowly. It was a start, but not enough. A smirk formed on Cain's face, and I knew I didn't have much time left.

The trees shot at me, at a speed that would have been impossible for anyone else to avoid, the Acacia trees' thorns poised to cause me pain. But one deep breath slowed everything down, so I could see Cain blinking in slow-motion. I doubled my efforts of pulling water from the trees, and stepped out of the way of the trees. Trails of water formed in the air behind me, originating from the trees whose leaves were now going from green to sickly yellow. The water formed a stream in the air that would follow me wherever I went, forming a ball that hovered over my head.

By the time the trees hit the spot I'd been standing at, I was already halfway across the street. Cain began to react, but it was too little too late. I drained the water from the trees on his side of the street before he could get them to do anything, and their brown dried-out leaves fell to the ground uselessly. In a last frantic attempt to delay the inevitable, he dropped to the ground revealing a drone with some kind of plasma gun pointed right at me.

I, too, dropped to the ground as the drone began to fire, but it mattered not. There was enough water in the air above me to fill a small water tank, and it came crashing down on both Cain and the drone, knocking them both to the ground. It was at that point where all my activity came rushing back at me, and I felt myself get thrust back to the world of normal speed, which allowed me to hear Cain coughing and cursing in full clarity.

"Give up?" I croaked.

"Fine," He responded, "But I demand a rematch, I'm choosing the next arena."

I stood up and shrugged, "Fine by me."

Janar

There was nothing more beautiful in the world than being in the sky, surrounded by multicoloured clouds bathed in the light of a sunset. My wings spread wide as I glided through the air, my purple scales reflecting the warm oranges and pinks of the light. I took in a deep breath and sighed.

"*Nothing can ruin this moment.*"

"***You still haven't hunted anything!***"

My muscles tensed up for a moment, and I groaned internally. Of course, I couldn't have enjoyed the moment for too long, The Lord of All Dragons just had to go and ruin it for me.

"*My lord, it's a beautiful moment to be enjoyed,*" I tried to reason.

"***You can't enjoy it if you die from hunger. Flying takes energy,***" My lord scolded me.

"Fine!" I snarled into the air, looking back down to the ground. The national park was spread out underneath me, and my eyes were instantly drawn to a limping antelope. It was surrounded by its herd, protecting it from predators. Unfortunately, these herbivores were only looking out for predators on the periphery, not from above.

I dove, my massive weight bringing me down to the ground in a staggeringly short amount of time. At the last minute, I flared my wings and stretched my hind legs out. My claws wrapped around the injured antelope's body, and then held it there as my full weight pressed it down into the ground, crushing its bones and killing it before it even knew what had happened.

The other antelopes scattered, but I ignored them, already flapping my wings to get back into the air, dead antelope in claws. Once back in the air, I transferred the carcass to my front legs and leaned over so I could eat while flying.

I'd gotten used to the taste of antelope over the years, overcoming my initial apprehension. Not like I'd had much of a choice, The Lord of All Dragons had previously forced my hand. Each time I heard the sounds of bones being crushed under my weight, and tasted the earthy and dry flesh of the antelope, I was reminded of that first time, that first kill.

My maw was salivating intensely, with flames running along the potent saliva to roast the meat while I ate it. Each drip of saliva was a risk, not that I was supposed to care if a globule of my spit set the savannah on fire. But I did care, making sure not to let any of my combustible saliva escape.

I flew over the city after I'd finished my meal. It was night, so my eyes were treated to the glittering lights of the city, which only served to confuse and irritate me somewhat. I was both a daytime and nighttime predator, so I was used to being able to see clearly at night, but the streetlights and other human-made sources of lights only confused me, making everything appear dull. My eyes were struggling to decide how much light to let in, so they kinda settled into a middle point.

Still, I scanned the ground for any signs of trouble. Part of my job as the only member of the Three Wings with said wings was looking around for trouble. Sure, Jacob could move fast, but I could glide around for hours and see a lot more at the same time. Even from so high up, even with the artificial light interference, all the details stood out. It was a routine, a very dull one.

But it had its moments. A movement caught my eye, and a strange reflection too. Focussing on the source of the reflection, I spotted a mirror being held up, aimed. The strangest part is that the mirror was aimed right at me.

"How strange."

I narrowed in on the location of the mirror and began to descend, all the while the person holding the mirror perfectly tracked me through the sky. Perhaps it was a fan, though I didn't have many of those. And I honestly preferred meeting villains than my own fans, at least the villains feared what I could do.

As I got closer, the mirror disappeared and the figure took off running. My instincts rose inside me, and I swooped down, heart racing at the promise of a chase. I saw flashes of movement in the dark streets below, and could make out the details perfectly. A long coat, a purple gas. It stood out to me clear as day, clearer since this guy was running through a place that had few human-made lights. Yet I could not see who the individual was.

But then the figure ran into an empty parking lot, head covered in a cloak and mask, surrounded by purple gas. I swooped down and landed in front of him. The wind from my landed caused him to stumble backwards, and he let out a curse.

"What are you doing out here in the dead of night?" I questioned, keeping my tone as neutral as possible to avoid scaring him off.

There was no verbal response, as the individual threw something at me. Expecting it to be a stone, I turned my head, since it was easier to deal with the draconic rage if I turned my cheek. You did not want to be the person who hit my snout with a stone.

But when the object hit my scales, it did not bounce off like I expected, instead bursting into thick purple fumes. I found myself coughing, and shaking my head to get rid of the gas. After some moments, I looked back at the parking lot, but the guy who'd thrown the gas bomb had disappeared. My vision was slightly blurry, which confused me, but I didn't have time to worry about that. Fighting the blur, I looked around for the guy. All I saw was the empty lot, and the empty buildings around.

Then I spotted him, lurking at the edge of the car park. As soon as he saw I'd noticed him, he ducked into the streets beyond. My instincts flared once more with a desire to give chase, and so I lumbered forward like a horse, tucking my wings carefully alongside my body.

There was just one thing that bothered me about the situation. The man had been wearing a cloak and a mask, and was built tall and lanky. But the person I was following, was not the exact same. He wore a tight shirt, cargo trousers. Sure, he had a similar build, but his face was uncovered. I hadn't gotten a good look at it, but it reminded me vaguely of myself, my human form, that was.

"Perhaps this is a fan…"

I decided I needed to play it safe, so I began to speak, hoping that Cain's invention wouldn't let me down. The little sunflower seed sized earpiece in my ear activated, at least, I hoped it did.

"I've encountered a strange situation, and could use some backup just in-case. Are you guys free?" I called through the earpiece.

<Sure,> Joshua replied soon after, his little voice in my ear. It was harsh, but I ignored how the sound hurt, <Where are you anyway?>

"Honestly, I don't know," I confessed.

<The earpiece has shared your location,> Cain informed us. He sounded tired and grumpy. Perhaps he'd lost a game of chess, or an invention was not turning out like expected. Such things happened from time to time.

"Cool, I'll keep moving then. See you in a bit."

The standard responses came in, and I shifted my focus entirely on the figure running away from me.

Janar

The guy was always two steps ahead, disappearing around another corner each time I managed to catch him in my sights. Every time I spotted him, he seemed to look more and more familiar, which was unsettling.

I was getting lost in the streets, losing count of how many turns I'd taken. But that didn't matter to me, since I knew I could always take to the skies to escape a situation if need be, even if the buildings and walls around me pressed in too tight for my wings. I had my magic, I could lift myself up.

I continued galloping along the empty streets, before hearing something that sent a shiver down my spine. The roar of a dragon, and a human scream. There was a new smell in the air that replaced the coldness of concrete, and that was the metallic scent of human blood. I rounded the next corner, and took in the scene in front of me.

It was like staring at two funhouse mirrors at the same time. First there was the human, missing an arm and running right at me. His face was unmistakeably mine, down to the bump in my nose and the slightly lazy eye. He was panicking. The thing was though, I could tell that this wasn't truly me. His nails were shorter, he actually had muscles, and he had a buzz cut. Ever since becoming a dragon, my human hair had been hovering around shoulder-length.

This wasn't my spitting image, it was a bastardisation. From him being taller to his tanned skin, he was a more traditionally masculine version of my human self. My vision became blurry again, and the antelope meat in my stomach complained, threatening to force itself out of my mouth.

"*W-what?*" I thought, trying to control my breathing and keep my body from swaying. Meanwhile, the man-me came to a halt upon seeing me, and stepped backwards into a trap I'd unwittingly set.

A larger, bulkier dragon than I had been stalking the man-me, and its jaws clamped around his waist, almost snapping him in half. Deja-vu ran through my mind, the bite looked very similar to what I had done to Margaret 3 years before.

She probably had an expression of shock and horror, since she was looking down at her midsection where I'd bitten into her. My teeth had easily pierced her waist, ripping through the juicy flesh. The taste was divine, I simply needed more. I pressed my torn paw against her and pushed, while pulling my head back. Most of her midsection was torn away into my maw, and the force of my efforts split her spine in half. Her screams were loud, but I ignored them as I began to eat. Her top half had fallen down into the mess of intestines and legs, her face smothered in the blood.

I shook my head, not appreciating the memory surfacing to my mind, especially since this dragon also looked similar to myself. It had the same purple scales with lime-green highlights, the same horn shape and the same eyes. There were some spikes though along its shoulders, which I didn't have. This dragon was bigger, more muscular and had a more powerful tail. Like the human, it seemed to be a more masculine version of myself.

I swayed, feeling lightheaded, which wasn't good. I could barely think as I watched the dragon-me eating the man-me, and began to back away, thinking I could escape the situation and wait for backup.

As I retreated, my tail hit a trash can, causing it to scatter along the ground. The pungent smell of trash filled the air, replacing the sweet blood, and the metal clattered along the concrete ground, the sound echoing against the apartment buildings around. The dragon stopped eating and looked at me, growling slightly. Eerily enough, the man-me was also staring right at me, despite the missing chunk in the middle of his body.

"Shit," I whispered. Both the dragon and the man-me began to move, running right at me with terrifying speed.

"NO!" I screamed, backing out of the street and running away for dear life. I could hear the two behind me, the lumbering of the dragon, and the skittering of the man-me. Glancing back, I saw the two running side by side. The man-me was on 4 legs, his spinal cord just barely hanging on despite the skittering. He moved like an insect, scuttling alongside this larger beast who'd just been eating him a few moments before.

The sight was too much, I let out a shrill roar of fear and turned back to keep running, not even realising that I didn't know where I was running to. Not even caring. All I could do was run away.

Jacob

I arrived at the scene first, at some empty parking lot. There was a strange mist in the air, though I couldn't make out exactly what it was due to the darkness of the night. Oddly enough, there were few streetlamps in this part of the city. I filed that note away as a potential recommendation to the governor, or an investment to make on my end.

<Janar's on the move,> Cain informed me.

"Yeah, I know that," I responded sarcastically.

<No, he's like... running. Fast.>

Then I heard the strangest thing. A roar, high-pitched in a way that I seldom heard. It was unmistakeably Janar's roar, but still peculiar. The hair on my arms rose, and my neck felt cold.

"I think Janar is in trouble," I told Cain.

<You might be right. Follow his movements, I'll be there soon to help. Just gotta get Dan all started up->

I ignored Cain speaking about his car and brought out my phone, which usually wrapped around my wrist like a bracelet, unwrapping into a fully-fledged super-modern device whenever I needed it. Cain could work on whatever his car project was all he liked, he could even call the machine 'Dan' for all I cared, because he allowed me to have some of the coolest things imaginable. No hero group around the world had anything close to what we had, partially because they stubbornly refused our help.

I opened the tracker software that Cain had installed, and began running along, following the path that would take me to Janar. It was a maze of streets, and Janar seemed to be going around in circles, which would only make him easier to find, I reasoned. Stepping into the shadows of the buildings, I began to navigate my way towards him.

After I got around halfway towards him, I heard a strange sound. Water trickling. Looking up from my phone, I noticed a small stream of water running across the street. I wouldn't have paid it much mind, if it weren't for the fact that the water was not just running on the street, but upwards and sideways across the nearby walls. Such a feat was just not possible, unless powers were involved.

My curiosity got the better of me and I let my phone roll back into a bracelet, while I approached the stream of water, making sure to walk carefully and quietly. I tried to get a sense for the water with my power, trying to find out what was causing the strange behaviour, but got no response. I hesitated, and tried again but harder this time. Still no response, I couldn't so much as sense the water like I normally could.

Whatever water this was, I had no control over it.

Cain

Dan pulled into the parking lot, and I took over the driving, manoeuvring him into an empty parking space. There were plenty of those, the whole damn lot was empty. The only reason I didn't let Dan park himself was because I was in a rush, so maybe later. There were few lights, just the moon in the sky, Dan's headlights and a couple of street-lights. There seemed to be some kind of gas in the air, possibly smoke. It blended in with the darkness, so I didn't pay it much mind.

Even inside the car, I could hear the distant roaring of a dragon. This certainly got me out of my Jacob-caused stupor, as I knew that if there was an angry dragon on the loose, I would be the one to stop it, or him, from hurting anyone. Slinging my power removal device onto my back, I leapt out of the car, and ran towards the maze of streets beyond the car park.

Once I entered the darkness of the streets though, all sounds ceased. I could no longer hear the dragon's roars. In fact, I couldn't even hear the breeze in the air. It felt very lonely.

"No matter," I muttered, "That's what the earpiece trackers are for!"

I brought out my phone, and checked the trackers. My heart skipped a beat as I saw something that shouldn't have been impossible. The map was blank. I couldn't see where Janar was, nor Jacob. Thinking that it was a bug, I reached in with my power and forced the software to register the trackers.

Nothing happened. Sure, the software responded, but nothing changed. I was breathing heavily now.

"No, no. It's fine," I reasoned, "This is just a crutch after all, I have the power to do this myself."

I channelled my senses outwards, using my nature and technology powers to feel through any nearby pieces of technology, or bit of nature that so much as imitated a DNA sequence. But moments later, I felt it. Or rather, felt the lack of anything. It was as though my powers had stopped working.

Panic was definitely setting into my heart now.

"Hey guys?" I called into the earpiece. There was no response. I tried again, over and over to no avail.

It began to dawn on me that I was truly alone. And there was no way to know why. Reasoning escaped my mind, and I began wondering why I wasn't getting a response.

"No, perhaps it's just something jamming my powers for now. I have to go search for them!"

Steeling myself, I took a good look around me. The street itself wasn't anything fancy, barely enough space for two cars to pass by and no pavement. Walls lined the streets, marking out the area where the street ended and the buildings began. Those buildings appeared to be residential, as I could see frequent windows, curtains, and beds. But no lights were on, and clearly not even copper wires had been installed, since I couldn't sense those. So these were apparently empty, yet fully constructed. I began to run, calling out into the air, "Janar! Jacob!"

I ran through the streets like that, calling for my friends over and over. Each corner that I turned revealed more empty street, and each empty street somehow felt lonelier than the last. That was it, the thing that shook me to my core. I was alone, truly alone. Not in the way I isolated myself within the Tower X, knowing my friends were close. No, I felt alone in the same way

I felt once my parents had forgotten about my existence. And particularly in the same way as when Peter had left me in a jungle to die.

But still I ran on, hoping to defy that loneliness. Fearful of what would happen if I stopped moving.

Jacob

I peeked around the corner and saw some vague figure lit up by the moonlight. He was facing away from me, contemplating his hand for some reason. But then I saw it, the trickle of water that ran up his arm, and the liquid ball that swirled above his open palm. Strangely enough, he wore a fedora to match his short-sleeved shirt and trousers. I couldn't make out more details than that, despite the water that reflected the moonlight.

For some reason, I felt compelled to approach the stranger. I was a few strides away when he spoke, a cruel undertone in his voice that sounded extremely familiar and made the hair on my neck rise.

"We meet again, Jacob."

My legs were glued to the ground as the man turned around to face me. Though his face was covered in shadow, I could still see who it was clearly enough.

"Patrick." My mind was swimming with emotions. Confusion about why I was seeing this guy, hatred at who he was, fear of what he could do. Suddenly, the world felt unsteady.

"Ah, so you recognise me," He laughed, "I hear that bitch is helping you with your little project."

"Don't speak about Electra that way," I snarled, though a part of me wondered where he'd gotten that information from. I assumed by my project he meant The Three Wings, but only Janar and Cain knew Electra was assisting us.

"I can speak about my property however the damn hell I want," he yelled, and the water that had pooled below him reacted, forming a spiky wave around him. I would have stumbled away, but I felt stuck to the ground, unable to move. My brain was still trying to reach out to the water, but it was not responding. Patrick had the power, I didn't.

"I can feel you trying, you know," Patrick grinned, "I've always been more powerful than you!"

"We took your power away!" I contested.

"I got it back."

"Impossible!"

"Oh yeah?" Water was now creeping around my legs, helping to hold me in place, while Patrick continued to taunt me, "Wanna bet? I know what you're truly afraid of."

I could hear a roaring, but not of a dragon. It was a roar of water. At the end of the street behind Patrick, a large wave of water emerged, rounding the corner. It was like a localised tsunami. The water at our feet began to swell as well, steadily rising.

"How sad for someone with water powers to drown," Patrick taunted, "Of course, I'm not going to let you die, I'll bring you back. And then I'll do what I promised, break you and that foolish girl too."

He laughed as his body lost its form, becoming like a liquid. His dark skin turned translucent, his clothes too, and he fell to the ground, becoming one with the current that swept at my legs. I tried desperately to move as the wave approached at lightning speed, but at the last second I took in a deep breath and closed my eyes.

One moment, I was standing upright. The next, my body was violently thrown back, and I felt myself get tossed around in the water for a while. My arms flailed, legs kicking as I tried to swim up to escape being stuck underwater, but the current kept dragging me back down.

"You won't escape me," Patrick's voice was all around me, "I hope you enjoyed your final moments of freedom, toy."

Janar

I kept running, the dragon-me and man-me still hot on my tail, and my legs were complaining about it. My body had not been designed for long distance running, and I'd been running for a while. Fortunately, my lungs could keep up the effort, but still my muscles strained under the pressure.

I turned a corner and spared a glance backwards, which turned out to be a fatal mistake. My legs hit something cold and hard, and I tripped, landing hard on the ground and tumbling. While I was rolling, I noticed the thing that had caused me to fall, a metal dumpster. I got back on my feet and staggered away, only to realise that I'd turned into a street with a dead end.

Trapped!

I whipped round as the dragon and man-me turned the corner, both slowing down as they instantly realised the position I was in. There was a dull pain in one of my legs, and so I limped backwards until my tail touched a wall, the end of the road.

"Shitshitshitshitshitshit..." I cursed, glancing wildly around me as the panic set in. It hurt to look at my pursuers, hurt in a way that I could barely even comprehend. I wasn't thinking clearly, so I felt as though I was unable to escape despite the open night sky above.

The dragon opened its maw and shot out a fireball, which I ducked to avoid. I could feel the heat as it sailed over my body and crashed into the wall beyond, and that fact made the entire situation worse. I couldn't remember the last time I'd felt anything warm.

I tried to shoot back a fireball of my own, but it fell short and hit the ground. At that moment, the man-me scuttled across the road towards me, and I let out a loud screech and tried to jump backwards, which only succeeded in my slamming myself against the wall, which somehow held up.

"Kill it you fool!"

I tried my fire-breath, but the man-me dodged it, crawling alongside a wall, still scuttling towards me like a horrible insect. My muscles tensed up, and I shrank down, cowering.

"You don't cower! What kind of a dragon are you?"

I could do nothing. But my body started moving on its own, making me feel as though I was in the back-seat, watching someone else drive.

"I'll show you how to behave yourself."

The Lord of All Dragons took over my body and I went on the offensive, swiping at the man-me while breathing fire at the dragon, who responded in kind. My body took the flames, which felt hot yet did nothing. I noticed how some of the fire washed over the man-me and didn't affect him.

My body swiped at the other dragon, who wasn't quite fast enough to escape the attack, and my claws passed clean through. Except, they didn't draw blood, nor encounter any resistance. It was as though the other dragon wasn't even there. My tail swung at the man-me, and similarly just passed through without resistance. It was as though I was fighting the very air.

"Something's going on."

"It's taken your useless brain long enough to notice."

The masculinised versions of me still hurt to look at for some reason, but I was now detached from the chemical response that made it hard for me to think. I could not study them gain, and notice things. It was odd, as we we were all fighting with a ferociousness that would have shredded anything to pieces, but no-one was actually causing any harm.

I had to figure it out, and quick. I'd no clue what my friends were dealing with if it was this bad for me.

Jacob

I tried to fight against the flow of water, kept trying to swim, but I was continuously pulled towards the ground, as though Patrick himself was holding onto my legs so that I couldn't escape. I tried reaching out with my water power, but to no avail. I sensed nothing, I could control nothing. All I could do was hold my breath and hope, hope that somehow I would not drown.

The water roared in my ears, and the current pulled me and thwarted any attempts to regain control. I could barely keep myself afloat, and ended up swallowing more water than I would have liked. It was dark, I could barely see what was going on around me, but I felt the occasional bit of debris, a plank of wood, a tire. I tried to grab them, for leverage, but kept on missing.

I felt caught between reality and visions, as memories from the time Electra and I nearly drowned kept passing through my mind.

Some of the ground underneath Electra gave way, and she fell forward, right onto me. Electra desperately grabbed at me to hold on, but the sudden pull from her falling was too much, and my grip on the tree root gave way, sending us both into the river.

I could remember the feeling of being trapped in a strong current, unable to resist against the might of the river. It was horrible, since I knew at that moment that we could have been swept away to a whole different part of the country if it weren't for Janar saving us.

"Speaking of, where is this going to?" I thought.

"Does it even matter? Patrick is controlling it."

My lungs were screaming at me now, and the temptation to take a deep breath grew stronger and stronger. I knew that I didn't have long left until I died, or worse. In that moment of desperation, I remembered the futility of fighting Patrick previously, and the reason I'd gotten trapped in the river in the first place.

I had no control over this water, and my speed powers never mixed well with water I couldn't control. But perhaps, just this once.

The tug of the current slowed, and I began to move, walking slowly along the ground against the flow of the water. The world around me was blurred between two realities, and as I moved, everything became less clear, and more confusing. I tried to push off against the ground, to surface above the water, but it still didn't work. I only succeeded at jumping.

Then I felt the current strengthen, trying to glue me back into place. I tried walking away, which was difficult at first as the current tried to hold me in place. But as I kept going, the current weakened, and I managed to settle into a steady rhythm. The surrounding water became darker, purple-ish in the moonlight. I waved a hand through it, and it swirled like a gas.

"*Huh?*"

I kept up my momentum, and the image of being trapped underwater faded away, replaced by a different scene altogether. A street, walls and buildings, and some kind of purple vapour in the air which grew less dense the more I walked. Unable to hold my breath any longer, I started to breath again, and water didn't fill up my lungs. A strange purple smoke left with every exhale, and more and more fresh air entered with every inhale.

I walked out onto another street and looked back, seeing a thick cloud of purple inching its way towards me.

"How strange, there's no water. Perhaps it was an illusion?"

Hope fluttered through my chest.

"Perhaps Patrick too was an illusion?"

I was free from the nightmare, for now. Since the purple fog was still approaching me, I knew that I had to keep a good distance from it, which could eventually drain me of my energy. So for now, I settled on a different goal. My phone unfurled, and I looked at the tracker map. There were two nearby points, Cain and Janar. Cain was closer, so I decided to head for him. Hopefully, I could do something to help him dispel the gas, and whatever nightmare he was facing.

Cain

My legs were tired, and I was still alone. It was cruel, there was no other way of putting it. I'd left my rational mind behind several street corners ago, and all that was left was paranoia and fear. And boy did those emotions get to work.

Something began to gnaw at my mind. I recalled the moment I'd spent with Jacob earlier that day, training. Was he testing me? Had I failed a test I didn't know about. Perhaps this was the Three Wings way of kicking me out, leaving me in some impossible situation to go mad and die. The worst part is that it was working. I was going mad. Perhaps, given enough time, I would die. I wanted to, at least. It'd be cruel if I couldn't.

I wandered on though, somehow being driven to keep walking despite it all. Stopping would be giving up, and I wasn't quite yet ready to do that. There was still some rational mind left, it seemed. But it was buried deep underneath the adrenaline pumping through my veins. I'd lost track of how much time I'd spent wandering around in search for my friends. But of course, if they were observing me, I would never be able to find them. Janar could turn invisible if he wanted. Jacob could outrun me and keep on the periphery.

But then Peter showed up again, finding me huddling by the fire, wrapped in a dead mans jacket but still shivering. And he laughed before he said a single word.

"Ah there you are Collins, I found you," Peter gloated, "You know, the others have been looking for you, but they think you ran off. After all, some money and spare tech has gone missing, so you could have just run off to start a business or something."

My hands were shaking, and I couldn't stop them.

"How strange that my powers aren't working," I reasoned in the back of my mind, *"Perhaps I'm just in a bad situation to use them in?"*

After a while, I saw something that made my heart jump in my throat. It was someone's shoe... and their foot was still in it, chewed off. After a bit of looking around, I was able to track down some other articles of clothing, including another large jacket that had a small phone in it. It was a quite dated phone and barely functional, but it was still something.

A lightbulb went off in my mind, as I recalled what I'd done to survive the last time I'd been left in a place alone to die. At that time I had just enough technology on my person to make it through and out the other end. I'd learned from that experience.

I had found a lighter in a jacket pocket, but it was out of lighter fluid, probably all used up on the fire previously. So instead, I resorted to picking open the cell phone I'd found and combining it with some other bits to make something that generated sparks that I desperately hoped would catch on the kindling.

And it worked! I managed to get a small fire burning, and used a sharp bit of broken circuit board to cut open one of the mangoes to eat from.

Somehow, something caused me to forget the spare technology and plant matter that I kept in my pockets at all times. It was for that reason that I wore clothes that had lots of pockets, despite the fashion atrocity I committed. A shirt with two chest pockets. A blazer. Cargo pants.

My hands dived into my pockets, pulling out chunks of circuits, wires and seeds, and I felt my connection to them. These bits and bobs, junk to other people, were a part of me. I could feel it. The circuits began to move, reshaping themselves. The seeds grew along the circuitry, merging with wires and growing strange copper-tinted leaves. My powers were working! There was hope!

A little device formed in my hands, and I cupped it very gently. When it was finished, I began communicating with it, through my power as opposed to with my senses. There was a suspicion in my mind that I couldn't yet trust those senses of mine.

"What is going on? What does my environment look like?"

I got a response, a mental image. The device, with its improvised camera, could not see me clearly. There was something in the way, something dark. I frowned, and put in effort to improve the camera. My will dominated the poor component, and forced it to make generational leaps until it was the single best camera currently on Earth.

The mental image improved, and switched to a live feed so I could see any changes. I aimed the camera at myself, and still got nothing. My heart fell, and I let out a sigh.

The most important sigh of my life.

There was a flash of movement when I sighed, the darkness shifting slightly. My eyes widened, and I breathed out as hard as I could. For a brief moment, my eyes saw purple darkness, and then the street came back into view. But my camera's feed was clear and hadn't been affected, there was something purple in the air. Some kind of smoke or something.

"Now I know what I'm fighting against!" I yelled. Immediately, I got to work. More seeds poured out of my pockets and began to grow, and I shaped them to suit my will. Minutes passed by, but I was patient. Steadily, as my plants grew and began to suck up the gas, the world around me became blurred between two images. Several minutes later, I could see clearly again, and I suddenly felt as though my lungs were clearer as I breathed in fresh city air.

Jacob was standing in the distance, mouth agape. He jogged up to me and tackled me into a hug.

"Oof!"

"Cain! You're okay! How did you clear the gas?"

"With... plants... of course," I responded, referring to the ring of purple flowers that now stood in a circle around me. I patted Jacob on the back, and he let me go.

"Well, that's fantastic! Quick now, we've gotta help Janar, and track down whoever's responsible for this gas."

"Right, wait, hold on," I pinched the bridge of my nose, "That's too fast. Can I process things for a bit? I just had the most horrible time."

"Same here," Jacob frowned, "Which means that whatever nightmares we've just been through..."

It didn't take me long to realise what Jacob was implying. My eyes opened wide, "Janar!"

Janar

It was strange, watching my own body fight while I observed in the back seat of my mind. Like I was playing some kind of video-game and someone else took control over the character. The advantage was that I could now notice what was going on. I could see how the dragon-me and the man-me dealt no damage to the real me, and how I in turn didn't do anything to them. Everything just kinda passed through like it wasn't there.

Which, of course, led to one conclusion in my mind. It had to be some sort of illusion, a trick being played on my eyes or in my mind. I tried to sense around for what I did have control over. First, I attempted to wiggle my ears, move an eye or even so much as cause a muscle to tense up. But that led to a whole load of nothing, save for one thing. I did manage to get a hold of my power, and channel a tiny smidgen of Aether into a spark. Somehow, I still had control over my powers – perhaps it was separate in some way from my physical body? Or maybe my lord had left me control over it. I would have to figure out a way to speak to Cain about the problem later.

Either way, I was free to use it, so I began wondering what on earth I could do to dispel whatever illusion I was under. It would be difficult without knowing how the illusion worked, and getting that information would use up my valuable and limited energy.

"Or maybe, just maybe, I don't need to know how the illusion works?"

I considered my options. The cleanest route was identifying what power was being used against me, and developing a specific counter-measure for it. That would take the least energy, but wouldn't be useful in the future.

I preferred the idea of just neutralising all illusions, so I would never have to deal with something like this again. The problem was that I wouldn't know how much energy that would require until I did it, and would probably result in me collapsing from exhaustion anyway.

A solution presented itself in the form of a mini-Cain in my mind. I could just permanently dispel this specific illusion, no need to identify what it was. He was always saying that powers required creativity, since they could behave in very vague ways.

With that in mind, I pulled at my power, the energy of the Aether that ran through me, and began to shape it with my intention. The process of doing so was always a strange one, especially for something I'd never done before. I just needed to have my intention clear in my mind, and like a baby discovering its fingers for the first time, the way forward would present itself. At least with powers I used frequently, I could manipulate them with precision. This would be about as precise as a 1 year-old using a spoon. It was also guaranteed to be tiring.

My magic flowed out, through and around me. One moment, my body was fighting a dragon and weird man-thing, the next, I was alone amongst a thick cloud of purple. Back in the driver's seat, I froze, taking in my surroundings. Then I sneezed, and purple gas flowed from my nostrils. The realisation struck me, and I wondered why I hadn't caught on sooner. This was the same gas that had engulfed me when I faced down that strange character earlier.

<Janar! Janar! Are you there?> Jacob yelled through the earpiece. I winced, my ear involuntarily twitching at the sharp sound.

"Yeah, barely, are you okay?" I responded, "Listen, there's this weird purple gas afoot, avoid it at all-"

<We know,> Cain interrupted, <We wanted to make sure you're safe.>

"I'm fine, I think. Might not sleep well tonight."

Jacob laughed, <Neither will we. Should we head to your location?>

"Don't bother. I think there's someone who is creating this gas, the guy I spotted when I called you. He shouldn't be too far, we gotta catch him and see what his deal is," My legs felt weak, but despite that I started walking to get clear of the gas. I tried to open my wings, but I had to be very careful since I didn't know what was around me. I felt blind, and I was too weak to lift myself into the sky like normal.

<If you say so, let us know when you've got eyes in the sky,> Jacob said, <We'll be here recovering our strength and following where this gas seems to be coming from.>

It took me a few minutes of walking to get clear of the gas, and I found myself in an empty playground surrounded by apartment buildings. The play structures were metal and rusted, dust and debris having built up around over time. Thick plants had grown over the entire playground, but it was still easy to see the shape of the little house and slide, and the monkey bars. There was still purple gas here, but it wasn't as thick, so I could see clearly.

Most importantly, I could stretch my wings and see the sky. I coughed, clearing my lungs as much as possible before finally spreading my wings and taking off, flapping hard. The gas swirled and was blown away by the gusts of wind created by my wings, until I'd finally gotten back into the air, into my element.

I glided around above the empty buildings for a while, looking for any hints of the guy, before finally giving in to the reality of the situation. There was only one thing that could help me identify the man, and though I was low on energy, I figured I'd have enough strength left to pull this off.

My eyesight shifted, and the world below turned into a dark grey, and monotone. The only details that stood out were vague edges of different structures, like black lines. Well, that and something else, something which I was looking for. Three yellow glowing points stood out amongst the grey, visible even if they were supposed to be covered by buildings. Large sources of Aether. Two of the sources were right next to each other, which I assumed to be Cain and Jacob. So instead, I focussed on the third one.

"Alright guys, I've got him in my sights."

Cain

With Janar's help, Jacob and I navigated through the confusing streets of purple gas, a ring of flowers around both of our necks that were working full-time to suck up the gas and replace it with clean air. The flowers had changed colour, originally being white, but they were now purple. Progress was slow, but steady.

After an hour of walking, we finally reached a destination. It was a large shack, possibly a garage or something, from which the purple gas flowed freely. I glanced at Jacob, who was inspecting the situation deep in thought.

"I think we should do something about the gas, would getting a ring of those flowers around the shed help?"

I nodded, "Most likely, but just to contain."

"Then get that set up, and then we'll go inside and put like, another ring of the flowers until the entire shed is nightmare gas free."

I got to work, throwing out my seeds and controlling them as they flew through the air, forcing them to make a loose ring around the shed. Jacob condensed some water around the seeds, so they had some nutrients from the air to work with. Moments later, my plants had sprouted and were hard at work clearing the air, growing flowers while they did so.

A flash of irritation ran through my mind as I glanced up at the dragon in the sky as his body passed through the light of the moon. Janar could have done this faster, he could do anything he wanted. I was stuck with two measly powers, forced to be creative in order to get any results.

"*Then again,*" I reminded myself, "*He does not have the same amount of energy as I do.*"

Within a few minutes, the air around the shed was clean, though more gas was seeping out of every corner of the shed, through cracks in the concrete and gaps in metal sheeted roof that let the gas through. I nodded at Jacob, and he became a blur that vanished from view before I could blink. I swung my head round to look at the shed, seeing again the blur that was Jacob opening the doors.

He retreated from the now open shed before the gas could reach him, slowing down as he returned to my side. The nightmare gas flowed out of the open-doors in waves, which my plants were barely managing to suck up. I threw out some more seeds, and more plants grew, stemming the flow of fumes.

The two of us approached the shed as I threw in more and more seeds, growing more and more plants. My legs felt heavier with each step, and my entire body felt stretched as though someone was pulling at every muscle in my body. Like there was a tiny black hole in every cell of my body, trying to eat me from within. I'd reached my limit.

The shed was clear now though, revealing a figure inside. He was wearing a cloak like some sort of imitation of a detective, though it was a purple. He also had a black surgical mask on, the sides of which nightmare gas flowed out freely. Coupled with his skin, which was darker than mine or Jacobs, and his purple trousers, he looked like a shadow.

The man hesitated as he saw us, and charged right for the door, which happened to also be where we were. His fist was raised. Before he could get very far, a jet of water shot forth and knocked him off his feet, sending him tumbling into the ground and my now violet flowers, which scattered a purple powder onto the ground and onto him. His fist opened, and a couple of smooth black orbs rolled out before bursting into violet fumes that quickly got sucked up. I shrugged the power removal device off my back and pointed it at the man as my plants grew over him, holding him into place.

"We have some questions," Jacob stated, "Starting with what the heck your deal is."

"I wanted to see if it was possible," the man responded after a small while, his voice hoarse. "Could The Three Wings be taken down by some nightmares?"

"Disappointed by the results?" I teased.

"Not really. With enough time, or gas, I could have pulled it off. Hurt you real bad. Still could."

"Yeah right, buddy. You're not pulling this thing off again," Jacob said.

The man looked up at us, straining against my plants, "Escaping jail will be easy, it's how I got out of South Africa."

"Really?" Jacob urged him on, "Tell us more."

"It's simple really, my power makes people see their worst nightmares, as you know," He smirked, "It makes them real. Not just seem real, but make them real enough to you that they can hurt you. So long as you believe in the nightmare, it can kill you."

"I see, so it all depends on keeping that illusion up long enough for the victim to die," I noted.

"Exactly! I didn't get you this time, but mark my words, my nightmare will become strong enough to off you. It is inevitable."

"I think he may be the cause of those deaths in the countries south of us," Jacob whispered to me, "The ones where the victims died of heart attacks. Bunch of heroes too."

"Huh?" I responded.

"You don't... never mind, I guess it was something I spoke about with Electra."

"So, are you going to cart me off to prison now?" the villain asked, "Take the great Dream Eater to rot in a cell? I know you don't kill your villains, so I'll come back stronger than ever, ready to eventually kill you."

I aimed the power removal device at the villain, "Hate to break it to you, but we don't work like that. You will never use your power again."

"B-but, you don't use guns!" He protested, eyes wide.

"That's right. But we do use this," I showed him the power removal device. It vaguely looked like a sci-fi rifle, but not wholly. For one, the frame was more wood than metal. For two, the opening was too large to fire bullets, since it had never shot a bullet in its entire existence. It was big and heavy, and included a stock that wasn't necessarily needed but did contain the chamber which would hold the results of its use.

"That's just a gun," the villain pointed out.

"This is the power removal device. I never gave it a different name because I like good, clear names. It's thanks to this why this city is not devolving to chaos like the rest of the world. So, say goodbye to your nightmare mist, it's never coming back."

Panic entered his eyes, and he struggled some more, trying to free one of his arms. I fired just as he managed to free his arm, a multicoloured beam shooting forth and connecting to the man and beginning the bright process of removing his power. He tore the mask off his face and released a large plume of the nightmare gas at me, which swirled around the colour-changing beam. However, the flow stopped as his power was taken away, and the plume was sucked up by the flowers on the ground and around my neck before it could get to me. The power removal beam faded, leaving behind the after-image of the great nothing filled with bright yellow Aether.

The man dropped to the ground, falling asleep. I heard a click from the power removal device as a new power crystal was dropped into the storage chamber in the stock. Another villain defeated.

Jacob

We sat around the dining room table in the old house, which had been practically consumed by the Tower X. Janar was in his human form, and Cain brought himself and nothing else. It was always nice seeing Janar as himself, even though there were subtle things that were off about him. I remembered his eyes used to be golden brown, but over the years they'd been overtaken by lime-green specks. A proper meeting room was still due to be built, but we hadn't gotten around to it yet, so the bare-bones table it was.

We were all staring at the crystal on the table between us. I didn't know about the other two, but flashbacks from the nightmare I had played in my mind over and over just by staring at the crystal. I felt as though I was drowning again, barely managing to hold my breath as Patrick tried to have his fun with me.

The crystal itself reminded me of a large amethyst, something that I could comfortably grip in my hand. It was a darker purple though, and was a perfect octahedron. Unlike other power crystals, the form was a little vague since a purple mist hung around its edges, like the nightmare gas that the villain had used.

"Did you guys sleep well?" I asked, breaking the silence.

"I didn't sleep at all," Cain confessed, which explained his dark eyes and vacant expression.

"I actually slept about as well as I usually do," Janar remarked. I didn't know if that was a good or bad thing.

"Well then, where should we store this one?" I continued.

"I'll keep it in my personal collection, to study," Cain suggested.

"Off the record then, got it." Then I chuckled darkly, "We should go to therapy. You know, just in case. I mean we all saw terrible things, but that's only because we've been through terrible things, so maybe it won't happen again if we've fought our inner demons and won?"

"Hell no," Cain protested, "That would just be a waste of my time. Don't worry, I've got myself sorted. I read the books."

"Rrrrriiiight," I was doubtful of his confidence, but decided not to pursue the matter further.

"I can't. Poor therapist would probably need therapy," Janar said. He took in a shaky breath, "And besides, I just... can't... go."

His expression loosened, and his eyes became vacant, even though he was looking at me. He just, wasn't focused on anything. It was a look I'd seen often, but it creeped me out whenever it happened right in front of me. It was as though, for a moment, Janar wasn't with us.

"Well then," I clapped a singular time, "Good meeting. I expect everyone's reports by the end of the week so we can clear things up with the police. Does anyone have anything else to mention?"

"Yeah," Cain rose up, "When they investigate the scene, let them know that any remaining flowers are potentially risky. I'll deal with them soon."

"What does that mean?" I questioned. In the corner of my eye, I noticed Janar shake his head as he was brought back into the present moment. He stood up to leave, stiffly waving goodbye to us. I waved back, but Cain didn't notice or didn't care.

"The flowers seem to have a nightmare pollen, I studied them last night. Could be interesting, especially if I can get them to develop the pollen without the nightmare gas. Who knows, could be useful."

"Can it," I ordered, "We are not using nightmare gas on other people."

"Just a thought, I'm not advocating for others to suffer like we did. I just... maybe there's a way to take the nightmare out? Like, make it some sort of dream gas. Doesn't seem useful, but it could be a way to subdue villains in jail. Not for us of course! But the other hero groups aren't any closer to using the power removal devices, at the cost of their countries. Maybe they'll accept this?"

I considered Cain's proposal, and knew that I could do nothing to stop him. Besides, the idea was mildly intriguing, especially if it could help ease the worlds suffering. "Fine, but don't forget to come out of your cave once in a while."

"Alright," Cain gave me a weak grin, "Maybe I'll beat you next time we train."

I laughed, "Fat chance!"

Janar left the room, and Cain made to leave as well, mumbling a good night. He took the crystal with him, and didn't even bother to inspect it like he normally would. Maybe he really was so exhausted, or maybe he didn't want the nightmares of the crystal to torment him.

They left me alone in the room, and I blinked in surprise.

"Oh," I mumbled, "I'm alone again."

Back to square one, with nothing interesting to do and Electra no closer to returning. It was worse now, though, since I did have one thing I could do to pass the time. Paperwork.

What a nightmare.

Don't miss out!

Visit the website below and you can sign up to receive emails whenever Janblu Iden Ayre publishes a new book. There's no charge and no obligation.

https://books2read.com/r/B-A-DJGNC-ZYPBF

BOOKS 2 READ

Connecting independent readers to independent writers.

About the Author

Janblu Iden Ayre is an individual of many interests, not just writing. They've been known to film, edit videos, draw and create video games. However, writing has been one of their longest passions ever since dreaming about turning into a white tiger and wishing to turn that into a book. Janblu has been trying to write a series about a small group of superheroes for close to a decade, though only recently have they found a direction they are satisfied with, "The Three Wings"

Read more at https://ko-fi.com/janbluthederg.